TWIRLY
WHOOPS!

KU-721-719

04534458

HarperCollins *Children's Books*

Twirlywoos and all related titles, logos and characters are trademarks of DHX Worldwide Ltd.
Copyright © 2018 Ragdoll Productions Ltd and DHX Worldwide Ltd.

First published in the UK in 2018 by HarperCollins Children's Books,
a division of HarperCollins Publishers Ltd, 1 London Bridge Street, London SE1 9GF

1 3 5 7 9 10 8 6 4 2

ISBN: 978-0-00-829726-8

Pencil, rubber and sketchbook © Shutterstock
Written by Emma Drage

A CIP catalogue record for this title is available from the British Library

No part of this publication may be reproduced, stored in a retrieval system or transmitted
in any form or by any means, electronic, mechanical, photocopying, recording or otherwise,
without the prior permission of HarperCollins Publishers Ltd.

www.harpercollins.co.uk

All rights reserved
Printed in China

MIX
Paper from
responsible sources
FSC™ C007454

FSC™ is a non-profit international organisation established to promote
the responsible management of the world's forests. Products carrying the
FSC label are independently certified to assure consumers that they come
from forests that are managed to meet the social, economic and
ecological needs of present and future generations,
and other controlled sources.

Find out more about HarperCollins and the environment at
www.harpercollins.co.uk/green

It's the Twirlywoos!

What have they found?

It's a
sketch book!

It's the
hooter!

WHOOPS!

The Twirlywoos are
stuck in the book!

Can you help them get out?

Try
SHAKING
the book.

The Twirlywoos
are still stuck.

Blow harder!

WHOOPS!

That didn't work either.

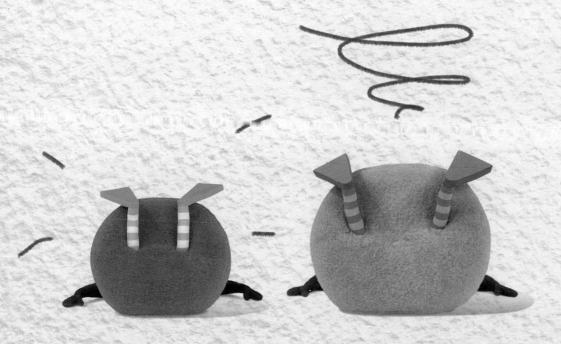

The Twirlywoos have
fallen over!

What will
they do now?

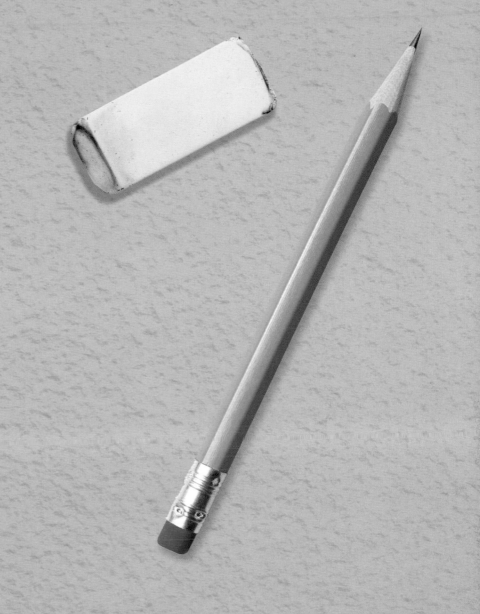

Clever Toodloo!
Back to the Big Red Boat,
Twirlywoos!

Bye-bye,
Twirlywoos!